Reborning

by Zayd Dohrn

A SAMUEL FRENCH ACTING EDITION

SAMUEL FRENCH

FOUNDED 1830

SAMUELFRENCH.COM

MUSIC USE NOTE

IMPORTANT BILLING AND CREDIT
REQUIREMENTS

REBORNING premiered at the Public Theatre as part of the Summer Play Festival in June 2009. The performance was directed by Kip Fagan, with sets by David Evans Morris, costumes by Jessica Pabst, sound and video by Leah Gelpe, and lighting by Matt Frey. The cast was as follows:

DAIZY	Greg Keller
EMILY	Ally Sheedy
KELLY	Katherine Waterston

CHARACTERS

KELLY - female, 20's.
DAIZY - male, 20's.
EMILY - female, 40's.

SETTING

A doll-maker's studio in Queens, NY.

To Dalin and Light

SCENE 1

(An industrial loft lined with shelves of dolls – some hairless, some without eyes, others just gray plastic casts.)

(The near-finished dolls are incredibly lifelike, photo-realistic. In fact, each doll has a snapshot of a real baby taped to its shelf, like a label.)

(There's a hallway leading to another studio, a bathroom, a kitchenette, and a freight elevator door. Also a couch, a computer, a TV, and a drafting table.)

(Music comes from the computer. Maybe Schooly D or the Beastie Boys.*)

*(A half-dressed young woman, **KELLY**, sits at the table, smoking a joint, wearing latex gloves, mouthing the lyrics.)*

(A dozen photographs of a baby boy are tacked above her desk – a set of Genesis Heatset paints, stencil creams, brushes, and a kit with tiny compartments for hair, nails, and eyes, all within easy reach. Also several beer bottles and containers of prescription medication.)

(A camera with a macro lens is mounted over the table, wired to a digital projector pointed at the wall.)

*(**KELLY** glances up every few seconds at the projection, which shows an extreme close-up of a doll's glass eye, enlarged a thousand times, the carefully painted capillaries visible.)*

*(**KELLY** is micro-rooting an eyelash into its vinyl lid with a hooked needle and a tiny drop of epoxy.)*

---

* See Music Use Note on page 3.

(There is a loud squawk from the intercom.)

KELLY. *(calling into the next room)* Daiz?

DAIZY. *(offstage)* Yah?

KELLY. You want to get that for me, baby?

DAIZY. *(offstage)* What?

KELLY. You want to get that please?

DAIZY. Get what?

(She turns off the music.)

KELLY. You want to get the fucking door? Sweeheart? Thank you very much.

DAIZY. *(offstage)* I'm working.

KELLY. So am I.

(no answer)

So am I! Working.

DAIZY. *(offstage)* You're closer.

KELLY. Arrghh.

*(**KELLY** puts down her tools, takes a hit from the joint, and peels herself off the stool, checking her butt for vinyl marks.)*

KELLY. If this is FedEx for you again, man, I swear to God...

(She touches a button on the intercom.)

KELLY. What?

*(A **WOMAN'S VOICE** crackles over the speaker.)*

WOMAN'S VOICE. *(offstage)* Hello?

KELLY. May I help you?

WOMAN'S VOICE. *(offstage)* Yes. Is this "Little Angel Nursery"?

KELLY. Who're you looking for?

WOMAN'S VOICE. *(offstage)* I'm here for Eva.

KELLY. Eva?

WOMAN'S VOICE. *(offstage)* To pick up – Baby Eva?

KELLY. Oh...sorry. You're early.

WOMAN'S VOICE. *(offstage)* Yes. I had some time before work. I wanted to drop in and – check your progress. If that's all right.

*(*KELLY *buzzes her in.)*

KELLY. Shit. Daiz?

DAIZY. *(offstage)* Yeah?

KELLY. I'm smoking a joint out here!

DAIZY. *(offstage)* Cool...be there in a sec.

*(*KELLY *runs to the table and stubs out her joint in an ashtray.)*

KELLY. Shit shit shit...

(She gathers the empty beer bottles in her arms, dumps them in the trash, and turns on the track lighting, which illuminates the dolls like objects in an art gallery.)

(She pulls on a pair of glue-splattered jeans.)

KELLY. Did you fucking die in there or what?

DAIZY. *(offstage)* Got a little roll going...I'll be right out.

*(*KELLY *goes to her computer and scrolls through her music library while she frantically waves the smoke away with her free hand.)*

(She finds a song, clicks on it, and Brahms' Lullaby starts to play.)

KELLY. Know what? Forget it. It's all – under control...

DAIZY. *(offstage)* Awesome. Thanks.

*(*KELLY *finds a can of Febreze. She spritzes it around the room, tosses the can, just as the freight elevator doors slide open, revealing* **EMILY**, *behind the wire mesh.)*

*(*EMILY *is middle-aged, wearing a suit and heels, very put together. She carries an expensive purse.)*

KELLY. *(out of breath)* Hi...

EMILY. Hello. Kelly, right?

KELLY. Mrs. Palmer?

EMILY. Emily.

KELLY. Emily. Hey.

EMILY. So. It's lovely to meet you, finally, in person. After all the email, I start to feel I'm corresponding with a machine – "kt@littleangels.com".

(KELLY *pulls a canvas strap, lifting the wire gate.*)

KELLY. Come on in.

EMILY. Thanks. Nice place –

(*Her cellphone rings. She grimaces at* KELLY, *picks up.*)

EMILY. Yes? All right, Jan...it's fine...Tell them to wait...I'm on an errand. In Queens. "Queens" the borough? I'm just – Tell them I'm on my way. I'm breaking up, Jan. I'll –

(*She hangs up.*)

EMILY. Sorry.

KELLY. No problem.

EMILY. You don't have a secretary do you, Kelly?

KELLY. Me? (*glances around*) Uh. No.

EMILY. It's like my mother back from the dead, I swear. The nag.

KELLY. Hah...

(EMILY *takes in the room, sniffs the pot smoke.*)

EMILY. So...Is this a bad time?

KELLY. Nope. Perfect.

EMILY. Are you sure?

KELLY. Yeah. Just wasn't expecting you – until tomorrow, that's all.

EMILY. No, I know. I know. I couldn't wait. (*re: the doll on the table:*) Is that her?

KELLY. No. No, she's back in the oven. Drying.

EMILY. Oh. All right. (*indicating the other dolls*) So...is it okay if I look around then?

KELLY. Be my guest.

*(**EMILY** picks up one of the dolls, looks closely at its face.)*

EMILY. Incredible. Seeing them in 3-D. The pictures don't do you justice, Kelly. You're an artist.

KELLY. Ha.

EMILY. Really. You even get – the dry skin, you know? The blotchiness.

KELLY. Mm.

EMILY. And the little stork-bites too...must be fascinating work. Paying such close attention to people's faces, I mean, must give you such a –

KELLY. Headache, yeah...

EMILY. *(smiles)* Unique perspective, is what I was going to say.

KELLY. Well...I'm better, actually, on the pore level, Emily, you know – whole people confuse me. Would you like something to drink?

EMILY. No, thank you – could I see her now, do you think?

KELLY. Sure. Uh...I'll go make sure she's dry.

*(**KELLY** starts to go.)*

EMILY. The pictures were okay?

KELLY. Fine.

EMILY. I had to have the IT people scan them for me at work. Made me feel about a million years old. I told them what you said about the "*DPI*", but I have no idea what that meant – or whether they understood – They said something about "lines." I said, "No, *dots*," but...

KELLY. They were fine, Emily. Exactly right. I think you'll be pleased. *(beat)* So...be right back.

EMILY. Okay.

*(**KELLY** exits.)*

*(**EMILY** waits a moment, and then wanders around the room, looking at the dolls.)*

*(She smells the smoke, spots the roach **KELLY** stubbed out in the ashtray, picks it up, sniffs it.)*

(She takes the lighter, lights the joint, takes a hit.)

(After a moment:)

DAIZY. *(offstage)* Kel? You get rid of him?

*(**EMILY** exhales, looks around for the ashtray.)*

(offstage) Hope you're sitting down now, babe, because you –

*(**EMILY** hides the joint behind her back as **DAIZY** enters – cute, scruffy, a very realistic ten-inch dildo hanging out of his open fly.)*

*(He doesn't see **EMILY** at first.)*

DAIZY. – are looking at my best piece – *(He spots her.)* ever – Oh.

EMILY. Hello.

(He snatches the dildo out of his pants, hides it behind his back.)

DAIZY.. Hey. *(He laughs nervously.)* Wow. I'm really sorry...

EMILY. It's okay.

*(**DAIZY** looks for a place to put the dildo.)*

DAIZY. I didn't realize –

*(**EMILY** takes the opportunity to drop the roach in the ashtray.)*

EMILY. Nor did I...Emily, by the way.

DAIZY. Daizy.

EMILY. Daisy, okay.

DAIZY. With a "Z."

EMILY. Interesting.

DAIZY. Hippy parents.

EMILY. Pleasure to meet you.

DAIZY. Likewise.

(looking for something to say...)

EMILY. So, how do you know Kelly?

DAIZY. We went to RISD together. In college? *(singing the school song:)* "R is for the R in Rhodeislandschoolofdesign... And I is for the I in Rhodeislandschoolofdesign"?

EMILY. I see.

DAIZY. You?

EMILY. How do I know –

DAIZY. Yeah.

EMILY. I was referred.

(pause)

DAIZY. *(re: KELLY)* So, she went to get the –

EMILY. Yes.

DAIZY. Which one?

EMILY. Eva?

DAIZY. Oh. That's a good one.

EMILY. Oh good. Good...

(long pause)

DAIZY. *(starting to go)* So, I'll just –

EMILY. Great.

*(**KELLY** reenters, with Baby Eva. She sees **DAIZY**, **EMILY**, the dildo.)*

KELLY. Daiz..? What are you doing?

DAIZY. I apologized, already, honey. I was just messing around. I didn't know you had a customer.

KELLY. Emily...God, I'm –

EMILY. Is that..?

*(**EMILY** has her eyes fixed on the doll in **KELLY**'s hands.)*

(She reaches out to touch it, pulls back, gets hold of herself.)

EMILY. Is it all right if I –

KELLY. Oh, sure. Yeah. Careful. She's not completely dry yet. Around the eyes.

EMILY. Okay.

*(**EMILY** takes a deep breath. She reaches out and takes the doll in her arms.)*

EMILY. Huh.

(*a long pause*)

(**DAIZY** *pokes* **KELLY**'s *ass with the dildo. She pushes him away.*)

EMILY. God...

(*She takes a deep breath.*)

DAIZY. (*re: the dildo*) I'll just go put this away, yeah?

(*Nobody answers.*)

Sweet...

(*He exits.*)

EMILY. The little crust on her eyebrows. I haven't thought about that for...God knows. I didn't realize I still had that in my mind...

(*She takes a breath, pulls herself together.*)

I'm overwhelmed, Kelly.

KELLY. I'm glad. (*re:* **DAIZY**) Sorry, again. About –

EMILY. Please. Don't worry.

KELLY. It's his job, y'know. The...adult rubber and latex items?

EMILY. I gathered.

KELLY. He started this mail-order catalog? After graduation. Guys send in photos. Written measurements. Buy them for their girlfriends, as jokes, I guess. Or whatever. Hang them on the wall. Like a deer head.

EMILY. "Written measurements"?

KELLY. Yeah, you can imagine. We did a lot of twelve, fourteen-inch jobs.

(**EMILY** *laughs.*)

EMILY. I see.

KELLY. He hired me, right out of college. That's how I got good, you know, with the photo-realistic skin and veins. Hair. He's really very – good at it.

EMILY. I could see that.

KELLY. Anyway...It's like – building model airplanes to him now. He's so used to it, doesn't understand sometimes how offensive it could be, to walk in on somebody like –

EMILY. It's fine, Kelly. I'm not offended.

KELLY. Oh. Okay.

EMILY. *(re: the doll)* Her neck still looks a little wet to me...

KELLY. No, that's – Little babies stay moist, y'know, in the folds? Secrete a lot of oil. But you can touch her there. It's hard silicone gel. Just for visual effect.

*(**EMILY** examines the doll, smiling to herself.)*

(after a moment:)

EMILY. God, she's close, Kelly. Really, really close...

KELLY. Oh. "But"?

EMILY. No. No, I –

KELLY. Tell me. There's a "Lifelike Guarantee." If I missed something, I'm happy to fix it.

EMILY. Just – Just something about her – tone, I guess.

KELLY. Tone?

EMILY. Her skin looks – a bit too rosy to me. Somehow? I don't know.

KELLY. "Rosy."

EMILY. Pink. Or ruddy? Flushed, I guess is what I'm –

KELLY. Yes, I know what rosy means.

(beat)

EMILY. I'm sorry. I guess most people want that. Airbrushing. Enhancements?

KELLY. *(non-committal)* Mm.

EMILY. Make them look more – Gerber-y. Your website, with the pastel colors, the cherub logo. *(re: the music)* Brahms? No offense. That's not me.

KELLY. Good to know.

(She switches off the music.)

EMILY. I want her to be realistic. All right? Nothing fancy or cleaned-up, just...I hope I'm not offending you, Kelly. Talking like this.

KELLY. Not at all. Not at all, it's a relief, actually. To be so straightforward. I thought I was being realistic.

(She takes back the doll, looks at it.)

(DAIZY reenters, dildo-less.)

EMILY. I'll pay extra, of course, for your time. Whatever you think is appropri –

KELLY. You don't have to do that. It's part of the package.

EMILY. Money isn't an issue for me. As long as the quality is there.

DAIZY. In that case, maybe you'd like to browse around my studio for a little –

KELLY. No, she does not want to look at your – Daizy! God. *(to EMILY)* It's fine. Really. Customer is always...

(EMILY digs in her purse.)

EMILY. I brought an old videotape. If you'd like to take a look –

KELLY. That's all right.

EMILY. I think it'll help.

KELLY. I can't work off video, actually.

EMILY. No?

KELLY. Nope. People ask. Not enough detail. Even a freeze-frame in HD is much too grainy. I can't get anything off it.

EMILY. Okay, but you could see how she moved, at least, and what she looked like, right? Facial expressions, or –

KELLY. "How she moved" doesn't help me.

EMILY. No, but I mean – It might inspire you or – I'm no expert, but I assume Michelangelo Buonarroti didn't sculpt from photographs, did he?

DAIZY. In the sixteenth century?

EMILY. You know what I mean. Picasso then. Rodin.

KELLY. *(laughs)* I'm not Picasso, Emily. Or Michelangelo. And I don't think those guys would have used video tape –

EMILY. No, of course not.

KELLY. They preferred real life.

EMILY. Well, but "real life" isn't available here, is it?

(beat)

*(***KELLY*** *looks at her.)*

KELLY. Okay...Fine. *(She takes the videotape.)* No problem.

EMILY. Great.

*(***EMILY*** *stands.)*

So...I can't wait to see her, once she's done. I'm tremendously – encouraged, by what I've seen thus far...

KELLY. *(Nods.)*

EMILY. Well then. A week or so?

*(***EMILY*** *exits.)*

*(***KELLY*** *and* ***DAIZY*** *look at each other. He raises a pierced eyebrow.)*

SCENE 2

(The loft. That night.)

*(**KELLY** is curled up on the futon, still wearing her latex gloves, drinking straight from a bottle of red wine.)*

(Emily's home video is projected on the screen – old, scratchy, color-saturated footage of Baby Eva, in various places around the house.)

*(After a while, **DAIZY** pokes his head in from the kitchenette.)*

DAIZY. Popcorn? Milk duds?

(She barely acknowledges this.)

(He comes into the studio, eating.)

You getting anything off that or what?

KELLY. What do you think?

DAIZY. Cool. Betamax.

KELLY. May as well be.

DAIZY. Probably taped over an original *I Love Lucy* collection or something.

(He watches the projection with her.)

How old?

KELLY. I don't know. Eighties, maybe? Early nineties?

DAIZY. I meant the baby.

KELLY. Oh. Eight weeks? Maybe? Around that.

DAIZY. Cute.

(She shoots him a look.)

What? I can't think she's cute?

KELLY. No.

DAIZY. Got some milia there, on the bridge of the nose.

KELLY. I got that.

DAIZY. Little vascular stain on her shoulder too...*(beat)* Be kind of fun, don't you think? To have a real one around this place?

KELLY. No, I don't think that'd be "fun".

(**DAIZY** *picks Baby Eva up off the table.*)

DAIZY. Little Chuckys are starting to creep me out, Kel, I'll be honest with you. Feel like homegirl might get my putty knife from the desk in the middle of the night, and like –

(*He grabs a dildo, makes Baby Eva "stab" him several times.*)

Ree! Ree! Ree! Ahhh!

(*He takes Baby Eva's hands and pretends she is choking him.*)

(*He gasps, gurgles, falls to his knees.*)

KELLY. Move, motherfucker! I can't see.

(*He falls to the floor.*)

Put it back.

(*He returns Baby Eva to the table.*)

DAIZY. You used to laugh at shit like that you know.

KELLY. You used to be funnier.

DAIZY. I think this "job" is starting to mess with your head.

KELLY. I like it. It calms me down.

DAIZY. You don't seem calm.

KELLY. I am! Calm!

DAIZY. Yeah, okay…So what are you watching for? If it's not –

KELLY. She wasn't happy with it.

DAIZY. Mm. And you think this is gonna make her –

KELLY. I don't know. I'm not a psychotherapist. I want her to be satisfied, okay? As a customer.

DAIZY. Um. That lady needs more than a doll, honey. I hate to break the news, but –

KELLY. We've been over this.

DAIZY. And?

KELLY. These *are* dolls. People do buy them.

DAIZY. What, "collectors"?

KELLY. Yes. Some.

(He scoffs.)

(KELLY *picks up one of the dolls off the shelf.)*

KELLY. This one's a sixty-two year-old patent attorney and doll enthusiast. Douglas. All right? Lives in Florida. His wife, Estelle, thought it might be cute to have a little Dougie as part of his collection. For the retirement party.

DAIZY. *(trying to joke)* A sixty-two year-old male "doll enthusiast?" "Dope."

KELLY. That's not the point. People do collect them. For all sorts of reasons. *(indicating another doll)* And this girl's having her third birthday party next month. Her mom wants to remember her, as a baby. In three dimensions. Like taking a lock of hair I guess. Bronzing the first shoes, or – whatever. People are sentimental.

DAIZY. *(indicating the shelves)* And the rest?

(KELLY *pauses the tape. The projection shows a frozen image of Baby Eva.)*

KELLY. Why are you so hostile about this? It's a job, right?

DAIZY. You had a job.

KELLY. Oh. You're still pissed about me quitting.

DAIZY. Come on.

KELLY. You are.

DAIZY. Nothing to do with that. I mean – you were really good at it, okay? But this is –

KELLY. You need me to pick up the slack, I said I would. Give me a couple orders.

(DAIZY *shakes his head.)*

KELLY. What then?

DAIZY. Honestly? I find your new "work" a little bit – disgusting, Kel. No offense.

KELLY. Thanks.

DAIZY. Sorry. But it's like – we're on Oprah or something here, and these people think they're buying *some product* that's gonna make them feel better about like – *(imitating Oprah)* "You get a doll! And you get a doll! Everybody gets a fucking doll!" *(picking up a doll)* Look at this. Is this a perfect symbol for some kind of – post-feminist capitalist nightmare? "Realities of life too depressing for you, little lady? Go shopping! Who needs a career? Play with dolls!" I mean – women in Africa lose half their kids within a year, all right? To diarrhea! Know what they do? They get knocked up again. Right away. They don't have time to raise a baby made out of plastic!

KELLY. Okay, Bono.

DAIZY. I'm not saying. Jesus, can't you just – There's something really sick and exploitative about making money off somebody else's suffering, Kel. You don't see that? "Little Angel Nursery"?

KELLY. So this is my fault. Selling rubber dicks is a moral occupation, but dolls –

DAIZY. The people who buy my dicks don't talk to them! They don't talk to them, or take them shopping, or fall in love with them –

KELLY. They actually have *intercourse* with them. But that doesn't count, apparently, in your –

DAIZY. Physical objects. With practical functions. It's a completely different –

KELLY. Do you even know the definition of a fetish object, Daiz?

DAIZY. No idea, why?

KELLY. You never read Freud?

DAIZY. No, I went to RISD. I can't read.

(She laughs in spite of herself.)

Go ahead, school me, Professor. O ye who went to Connecticut Prep before slumming it with us retards in art school. What does Freud say about fetishes? I'm a penis expert. I should know this.

KELLY. That the castration anxiety caused when a kid realizes his mom has no phallus makes him fixate on inanimate objects to replace her missing genital.

DAIZY. Ah. Well, that sounds ridiculous and incomprehensible. It must be smart.

KELLY. It means people invest things with emotional energy. They become symbols of unconscious longings. Of what's missing. We respond to them, as though they're real. It's a coping mechanism.

DAIZY. I'm worried about you, y'know...

KELLY. Oh, God. Don't do that.

DAIZY. Seriously. You know we haven't had sex in a month?

KELLY. It hasn't been a month.

DAIZY. How long's it been?

KELLY. I don't know. A week or two? At the most. I'm not keeping track.

DAIZY. Well I am. Keeping track. 28 days, 3 hours, 46 minutes.

KELLY. That's not a month.

DAIZY. It is if it's February.

KELLY. It's April.

DAIZY. I've been thinking – Maybe we should pull the latex.

　　(beat)

KELLY. I like latex.

DAIZY. *(snuggling her)* Seriously. I think you'd make a super-hot mom.

KELLY. Oh my God, Daiz...That is the single least erotic thing you've ever said to me.

DAIZY. So what? You're just gonna reproduce asexually now? Like an amoeba?

KELLY. Who says I'm planning to "reproduce" at all? I'm not interested in replicating my fucked-up DNA. We've been over this.

　　(**DAIZY** *goes to the shelves, looks at the dolls.*)

(long pause)

DAIZY. Maybe we should be seeing someone.

KELLY. What "someone"?

DAIZY. A...shrink? I don't know. A sex therapist.

KELLY. A sex therapist. Did we get married? I thought only married people had to go to –

DAIZY. You got a better idea?

KELLY. Yeah. How about you stop making such a big deal about a little – slow patch? I mean – I'm not calling Dr. Ruth just because we haven't fucked in a couple weeks, all right?

DAIZY. A month.

KELLY. A month, whatever.

DAIZY. I wasn't thinking Dr. Ruth. More like...Jamie Buffalino? Dan Savage?

KELLY. You're gay.

DAIZY. No. No, I'm writing him a letter right now. "Dear Savage Love: I'm male, hetero, disease-free. Moderately attractive. Sensitive to a woman's needs. My girlfriend won't fool around with me because she's busy making babies out of *plastic*. I approached her with a nine-inch hand-sculpted dildo, on Valentine's Day, and got no reaction whatsoever. Is there something wrong with me, or my synthetic friend, or am I right to be worried? Sincerely...Sensitive Blue Balls."

KELLY. "Dear Sensitive. Maybe your girlfriend's just going through some shit right now and you should give her a little space and support instead of a big hassle all the time. Maybe everything isn't always about you men...P.S. 'Blue balls' is an urban myth invented by date-raping frat boys."

DAIZY. He would not write that.

KELLY. He would. That's exactly what he'd write.

DAIZY. I think he'd write, "Dear Balls: If she's that into dolls, maybe you should find one you both can enjoy.

(He mimes sodomizing one of the dolls.)

DAIZY. *(as a ventriloquist, in the voice of Pinocchio:)* I'm a real boy now!

KELLY. Yech.

DAIZY. *(in Pinocchio's voice:)* I'll never tell a lie again!

(nothing)

All right, fuck it. I'm going to bed. Just me and Chucky here. As per youge.

KELLY. I'll be there in a minute.

DAIZY. Yeah, right...

(He mimes her nose growing longer with the dildo, makes the sound effect.)

(He exits.)

*(After a moment, **KELLY** un-pauses the tape.)*

(She takes out a prescription bottle, gulps down a few pills with some wine.)

(She watches the projection.)

SCENE 3

(EMILY and KELLY at the table, drinking coffee.)

(KELLY is badly hungover.)

(EMILY has Baby Eva in her lap. She looks at the doll for a long time, turning it this way and that.)

(KELLY takes a shaky sip, watching EMILY over the lip of her mug.)

EMILY. The hair, Kelly – How do you...?

KELLY. It's mohair. From Australia. Micro-rooted into the scalp. I started doing it that way after – Some of the wigs would come apart when people tried to shampoo them, so...

EMILY. Wow. You have amazing attention to detail.

KELLY. Crippling OCD. I'm on medication for it. Would you like something to drink, Emily? A beer, or –

EMILY. No, thanks. I'm late for work as it is.

KELLY. OJ?

EMILY. Water's fine.

KELLY. You sure?

(KELLY disappears into the kitchenette.)

EMILY. Hey – would you mind if I asked you something?

KELLY. *(offstage)* Sure. Yes. I mean no.

EMILY . What made you start doing dolls?

KELLY. *(offstage)* Oh...a friend of mine asked me. If I could sculpt her nephew, when he was in the hospital. A couple years ago. She thought his parents would appreciate it, after –

(She reenters, with two glasses.)

And they did. So, it turned out to be like – an untapped market. Or whatever you call that, when people need something? Word spread. Pretty soon I was able to give Daizy my two dicks notice.

(They laugh, clink glasses, drink.)

(**EMILY** *winces.*)

EMILY. Whoah...

KELLY. Sorry. That's probably mine.

(They switch glasses.)

EMILY. Wow. You always start this early in the morning?

KELLY. No. Wednesday is my special day.

(The joke falls flat.)

EMILY. Mm...

KELLY. Anyway, I like it. It's soothing. The work I mean.

(beat)

EMILY. The woman who recommended you, you know...
Brenda? I met her at the Westfield Mall. She was uh –
pushing her baby in a pram. We sat next to each other
by the water feature. I congratulated her, how ador-
able he was, asleep like that, in his overalls. We got
to talking...It took me maybe – ten, fifteen minutes.
Before I realized her son had been born with a retino-
blastoma. Had died in the hospital, when he was two.
And that this *thing* in the nine hundred dollar stroller
wasn't asleep. Wasn't breathing. Wasn't even a real –

KELLY. I don't remember her. "Brenda."

EMILY. No? You must remember the child though. That
story.

KELLY. No. Not really.

EMILY. Your other customers don't talk to you about –

KELLY. No. They don't want to discuss it, usually. And
even when they do, they don't use those words, Emily.
"Died." "Cancer." There's a whole language of like –
tense shifts, and euphemism for people to – most of
my emails just say "I'd like to have a memento of my
baby Julia whom I loved and treasured..." Y'know?
Something like that? "Loved" instead of "Love"..?

(beat)

EMILY. I'm sorry. I don't mean to be pushy. I guess I just never expected to be doll-shopping, for myself, by the time I was in menopause, so...*(laughs)* I wondered how other people came to it. That's all. Morbid curiosity. Forget about it.

KELLY. I think it's – private. How people choose to deal with –

EMILY. You're right. I should be glad you're so – circumspect, I suppose. You haven't asked me –

KELLY. I don't want to know.

(beat)

*(***EMILY** *digs in her purse.)*

EMILY. I brought some more things – Eva's booties. Birth certificate. This – What is this, a teething toy? Something I saved. I don't know –

KELLY. Emily.

EMILY. What?

KELLY. What the hell am I supposed to do with this stuff?

EMILY. I don't know. Use it. For inspiration. It doesn't matter. I just thought you'd like to see –

KELLY. A birth certificate? How am I supposed to *sculpt* this?

EMILY. I don't know. I thought it might – You know, I don't believe in ghosts. I'm not – religious. But many cultures believe there's a powerful trace...energy left on personal objects?

KELLY. I don't work like that. I'm not a psychic. I use *photographs?*

EMILY. Sure. I guess I just thought – maybe the video would have given you a better sense of the eyes or something, but –

KELLY. The eyes?

EMILY. Yes. I mean, the lashes are so delicate. These little white bumps –

KELLY. Milia.

EMILY. The milia on the nose. So alive, it just – Makes the eyes feel a bit flat to me, that's all.

KELLY. Flat.

EMILY. Maybe there could be something more underneath it, you know? Some depth?

KELLY. Depth.

EMILY. Yes. Why are you repeating everything I say? Am I using improper terminology, or...?

KELLY. No, it's the right "terminology" or whatever, but – When people say "depth," Emily, what they actually mean is just – shadows. Vanishing points. Perspective lines. Painter's tricks.

EMILY. But in sculpture...it's 3-D, so –

KELLY. No, it's not. It's still – look. *(She picks up the doll.)* See? Our eyes don't recognize "depth" at all. All we ever "see" is shape and color projected on a flat screen, right? The retina? *(She moves the doll back and forth.)* What's sent to our brain is just two-dimensional data. The surfaces of things. It's only when those things start to move that we begin to think about space. Calculate that these flat images are rotating in relation to us, showing other sides. Moving closer and farther apart. We believe we're seeing depth, but we're not, really, just – collaging it together. Like an optical illusion.

EMILY. Well, it isn't working, yet. She still looks like a doll to me.

(They sit there quietly.)

I'm sorry to be so fussy. I'm not the kind of person, you know, who sends her dish back, at a restaurant. "I ordered well, not medium well." As though there's some objective measure. "Well." "Medium." It's just a steak. I know that. These things are relative, fine. She's just not the way I remember her, that's all.

KELLY. *(gently)* Memories change. Over time. Pictures don't. Trust me, this is what she looked like.

EMILY. No, it isn't.

KELLY. You think your recall is more accurate than a 35 millimeter photograph.

EMILY. It's different.

KELLY. Right. And I can't *sculpt* your memory.

(beat)

EMILY. Hey – can I ask you something else?

KELLY. Why not? The dam is broken.

(She gulps the contents of her glass, goes into the kitchenette.)

EMILY. Do you always work with the gloves on?

KELLY. *(offstage)* Yeah. Helps keep off dust and oil. Why?

EMILY. I'm no expert, obviously, but I would think it might help to have more of a – tactile sensation, while you're working?

*(**KELLY** comes back in, her glass full.)*

KELLY. Well, I can't feel anything anyway, so it doesn't really matter what I wear.

EMILY. What do you mean?

KELLY. I had an accident, as a little kid. My fingertips were burned off.

EMILY. Really?

KELLY. Yes. Really.

(She waggles her gloved fingers.)

EMILY. Must make your line of work difficult.

KELLY. No. I have to trust my eyes more. Makes for like – mechanical precision or something. I like to think it helps me focus.

EMILY. A sculptor who can't feel. It's like Beethoven or something, isn't it?

KELLY. If you say so.

EMILY. Hm. What happened?

KELLY. *(drinking)* With what?

EMILY. The "accident"? If you don't mind – talking about it?

KELLY. No. It's um. Kind of a long story though. Sort of grisly, actually...I don't think you'll want to hear –

EMILY. I do. Please. If you're willing.

(beat)

KELLY. Um...Okay. *(laughs awkwardly)* Well. When I was a baby, I was – left, by my parents. Abandoned or what-ever...wrapped in plastic and dropped in a dumpster in the Bronx?

EMILY. You're joking.

KELLY. No. Um. Somebody poured Drano and bleach on my hands. Trying to take off my fingerprints, which shows an inherited um...Meticulous quality, maybe... *(forcing a laugh)* And they stabbed me a bunch of times, with some kind of...Awl or screwdriver or something. So I lost a lot of blood. This – construction worker found me the next morning. Took me to a hospital. Saved my life.

EMILY. Oh my God.

KELLY. I know, it's – sorry. It's embarrassing to talk about, but –

EMILY. No, but I mean – What kind of a person would do something like –

KELLY. I don't know. A junkie maybe? A teenager? Somebody confused, obviously. And desperate.

EMILY. You read about these kinds of things in the news-paper I suppose, but you don't ever imagine it could happen in real life...to someone you know.

KELLY. Yeah, I was kind of famous, for a while. In *The New York Post.* "The Dumpster Darling". Sold a lot of papers for those assholes, which is probably my greatest regret...

EMILY. Huh.

KELLY. So. I was in foster care for a while. A plastic surgeon and his wife adopted me. I was fortunate. If I'd just been left on the doorstep of an orphanage like most kids, without being mutilated first – No gruesome tidbits for the tabloids. No sympathetic rich folk wanting to look like heroes at the country club. I might have grown up in state care like the rest of those bastards. Flipping burgers for a living. Instead, I grew up in Hartford. Got to go to art school. Life's funny.

EMILY. Well...it explains the work, I guess.

KELLY. You think so?

EMILY. It couldn't be a coincidence, could it?

KELLY. I don't know. The irony occurred to me, if that's what you –

EMILY. I think it's more than irony...

KELLY. What's *more* than irony? Irony's a lot.

EMILY. Just – as an artist, your subconscious bubbles up, is all I meant to –

KELLY. *(laughs)* I'm not an *artist.* Jesus. Can you stop with that? "Picasso"? "Beethoven"? It's embarrassing.

EMILY. What are you then?

KELLY. I don't know. A toy-maker? A doll manufacturer? An unhappy person with a weird hobby?

(beat)

EMILY. Well, thank you for sharing that with me. I'm sure it's a painful memory.

KELLY. It's fine. It's not a "memory" at all. Just a story I've heard a bunch of times about myself.

(She finishes her drink.)

EMILY. I hope you don't mind my pickiness, Kelly. About the eyes. I just want her to be as real as she can possibly be...I'll pay extra.

KELLY. I'm not asking –

EMILY. And I'm also – enjoying – getting to know you, a little bit...along the way? I appreciate you're spending the time...

(**EMILY** *leans down and kisses* **KELLY** *on the forehead.*)

EMILY. Thanks for the water. I'll come by next week. When she's finished.

(**EMILY** *exits.*)

(**KELLY** *sits there, with the doll.*)

SCENE 4

*(**KELLY** is at her drafting table, working on Baby Eva.)*

(We see a close-up of the doll's face on the projection.)

*(**KELLY** has the artifacts Emily brought – the rattle, the dress, the bottle – set up in front of her like a shrine.)*

*(**DAIZY** enters, with a pizza box.)*

DAIZY. Hey –

(She doesn't respond.)

DAIZY. Thought you might want to take a break.

KELLY. Not now.

DAIZY. If not now, when?

(He opens the box and puts it on the drafting table. Wafts some of the smell into her face.)

KELLY. Look – I'll make you a deal, all right? Give me forty five more minutes, and then we can –

DAIZY. Kel – You've been working on that thing for three and a half days now. Straight. I don't think you've slept –

KELLY. I have a deadline.

DAIZY. I haven't seen you *pee*. Or *snack* in like eight hours. Aren't you tired or something? Hungry?

KELLY. Not especially.

DAIZY. You're sweating.

KELLY. It's hot.

DAIZY. Listen...Jack Kerouak. I say this with big admiration, all right, for the manic psycho-artist *spree* you got going on here, but – you don't sleep anymore? You don't eat? You don't have sex. All you ever do is drink, take pills, and work, all the time? It's like you've channelled all your biological energy into this piece of fucking plastic here. It's scary.

KELLY. That's what artists do, no? Channel energy into their work? Isn't that your whole bullshit TA spiel?

DAIZY. If you have extra maybe. If you're some fucking beatnik savant, and you're just overflowing with juices to spare for the drinking and gambling and bisexual orgies...awesome. But not if you're just wasting away in your room like an anorexic hermit, Kel.

KELLY. I'm not anorexic.

DAIZY. You're skinny.

KELLY. Heroin chic.

DAIZY. That's not funny.

KELLY. It's not supposed to be.

(beat)

DAIZY. Don't make me call in Pam and Herb, all right? You want another intervention? Three weeks of in-patient detox? In Connecticut? Because I will go there.

KELLY. Don't threaten me, Daizy. I was joking! *(beat)* I'm not high.

DAIZY. Except for the occasional weed.

KELLY. Except weed.

DAIZY. And booze.

KELLY. Which is not a drug.

DAIZY. Yes it is.

KELLY. It isn't illegal.

DAIZY. Well, maybe it should be.

KELLY. Okay, Elliot Ness. Can I get back to work now?

DAIZY. Take a break. Eat some pizza. You'll feel better.

KELLY. I can't.

DAIZY. Why not?

KELLY. There's something missing.

DAIZY. Pepperoni?

KELLY. She isn't done. Emily's gonna be back here on Monday, and she's not fucking done!

DAIZY. What's "missing"?

KELLY. Something. I don't know.

DAIZY. People can always say "there's something missing," Kel. That is not what we former art school dropouts like to call "constructive criticism."

KELLY. It doesn't have to be "constructive." It can just be fucking true!

(beat)

DAIZY. I see what you're doing here.

KELLY. What am I doing?

DAIZY. With your little – surrogate mom operation.

KELLY. Don't try to psychoanalyse me, honey. You sound stupid. You don't even read Freud.

DAIZY. I watch Dr. Phil.

(KELLY groans.)

Come on, Kel. I see the way you look at her...when she gives you a compliment...*(in a faux British accent for some reason:)* "Oh, Kelly, you're such a genius! Your work should be displayed in the Museum of Metropolitan Artistiness with Michelangelo and Donatello and the rest of the Teenage Mutant Ninja Turtles."

KELLY. Fine. You want me to stop? I'll stop.

(She pushes away from the table.)

What do you want to talk about?

(He laughs.)

DAIZY. Come on.

KELLY. No, you wanted to talk. Say something interesting.

DAIZY. I never said I wanted to talk.

KELLY. Oh, that's right. You wanted to fuck. *(She starts to unbutton her pants, sits on the desk.)* Quickly. Get it over with, all right? I'm working.

(He looks at her.)

DAIZY. As flattering as that sounds...

KELLY. What then? I'm trying to finish! How hard is that to understand?

DAIZY. You have twenty other orders waiting! You're gonna miss your delivery dates, which you've never done before, even when you were partying like fifteen times a day. For what?

KELLY. I just want to satisfy my customer. Do a good job. Make something beautiful. Does that sound drug-addicted and insane to you?

(beat)

DAIZY. No.

KELLY. All right then.

DAIZY. So let me help.

KELLY. Good. Fine. Help. Where've you been?

DAIZY. So what's the problem?

KELLY. *(frustrated)* The fucking eyes!

(He looks at the pictures.)

DAIZY. Flaw in the cornea there.

KELLY. Yeah, I got that already.

DAIZY. Oh yeah. So you did...

(He looks at the projection for a while.)

Looks good. Meticulous. As usual. A jillion times better than I could ever do, so –

KELLY. But not "real" enough, apparently.

(beat)

DAIZY. Well, let's see –

*(He lifts the camera and points it at **KELLY**. The projection is filled with a close-up of her eye.)*

KELLY. What?

DAIZY. Nothing.

KELLY. What are you doing, Daiz?

DAIZY. Life drawing. Stop blinking.

KELLY. Baby eyes are different, stupid. Different size. Translucency. Blood vessels...

DAIZY. Yeah, but yours are "real," right? Makes a difference.

KELLY. *(teasing)* I hope you don't do this with your work.

DAIZY. Oh, I do. I do. At all times, one hand on the drafting table, one down the drawers.

(She laughs.)

(They watch her eye on the projection for a moment.)

DAIZY. Mm...

(He moves the camera down.)

KELLY. What are you doing?

DAIZY. Getting some context.

KELLY. I thought you were supposed to be helping me.

DAIZY. I am helping. Just forgot what live skin looks like, that's all...

(The projection is filled with her nose, her cheek, enlarged so that each pore is visible.)

KELLY. Come on, stop. You're zit-hunting now?

(Her mouth, her teeth. Her breath fogs the image for a moment.)

(He unbuttons her shirt.)

This is perverted. Seriously.

(He moves the camera down her body.)

KELLY. You're dirty.

DAIZY. Take off the gloves.

KELLY. Daizy...

DAIZY. Come on. No plastics allowed. Take 'em off.

(beat)

(She snaps off one of the gloves. Her hand is covered in white roping scars.)

*(**DAIZY** rubs her palm.)*

DAIZY. Mmm...Hot. Live. Clammy. Scars.

KELLY. *(embarrassed)* Yuck. Give it back.

DAIZY. No, it's nice. Feels like hard work. Mine too. Calluses.

KELLY. I can't feel them.

(He slides her hand down his pants.)

(She laughs, shakes her head.)

KELLY. Nope. You could be a Ken doll for all I can tell.

DAIZY. Want me to describe it for you? Give you a mental picture?

KELLY. Think you can?

DAIZY. With absolutely clinical precision. I'm a professional, remember?

KELLY. Go ahead.

DAIZY. All right then. Length: 15.74 centimeters –

KELLY. 14.7.

DAIZY. *(laughs)* 14.7. Whatever. Five millimeter circumcision scar traversing the frenulum...Ten degree leftward curvature. Girth: 11.04 centimeters...Rapidly...Swelling... To around...11.5...

KELLY. Okay, stop. I can picture it now.

(She kisses him.)

(He lifts her up onto the table, knocking Baby Eva off the table onto the floor.)

(He climbs on top of her.)

(Parts of their bodies are projected on the screen, so close-up they become abstract.)

(hair)

(skin)

(pores)

SCENE 5

(Nighttime. The room is empty.)

(After a moment, **KELLY** *enters, half-asleep, wearing one of Daizy's shirts.)*

(She goes into the bathroom, pees, flushes, comes back out rubbing her eyes.)

(On her way back into the bedroom, she notices the empty drafting table.)

(She double-takes, panics for a moment, searches frantically, before she finds Eva where she fell under the table.)

*(***KELLY** *picks her up, examines her face for damage, unconsciously clucking her tongue, like she's comforting a real baby.)*

KELLY. Shhh...okay...

DAIZY. *(offstage) (sleepily)* Kel..?

KELLY. Yeah?

DAIZY. What are you doing? Time is it?

KELLY. Nothing. Just thirsty. Go back to bed.

(She sets Eva on the table, turns on a work lamp.)

It's fine. I'll be right there...

SCENE 6

(The next morning. **KELLY** *is in the kitchen, making coffee.)*

(Eva is on the drafting table. The camera is off.)

*(***DAIZY*** *enters from the bathroom, sleepy and bed-headed.)*

DAIZY. Hey, baby...

KELLY. Hey. How're you?

(They smile shyly at each other.)

DAIZY. Sleep well?

KELLY. Mm. You?

DAIZY. Like I'd been shot.

KELLY. Ha.

DAIZY. That was nice.

KELLY. Yeah. It was.

DAIZY. We should wait a month more often, y'know? Felt like I was back in middle school. Repeated premature ejaculation.

(She laughs.)

(He pours himself some granola, a layer of Cheerios.)

DAIZY. Get me some breakfast...and I'm going back to bed for the rest of the day. Care to join?

KELLY. I got a better idea.

DAIZY. Yeah? What?

KELLY. Maybe we should go away for a while.

DAIZY. Away where?

KELLY. I don't know. Florida? Where do people go when they're not working? Hawaii?

DAIZY. Why?

KELLY. Because I'm in love with you, idiot. I want to take a honeymoon.

DAIZY. Holy shit. I knew I should have skipped the melatonin. Did we get married?

KELLY. Not yet.

(He looks at her.)

DAIZY. You're in a good mood, huh?

KELLY. I am, actually. Yeah.

DAIZY. What happened?

KELLY. *(lying)* I don't know. Woke up flooded with happy hormones. Must be your magic cocksmanship.

*(**DAIZY** laughs.)*

Or maybe the Zoloft's finally kicking in or something. Either way, I feel amazing, so...

(He looks at her carefully.)

DAIZY. Are you wired, Kel?

KELLY. *(disappointed)* No.

DAIZY. You sure?

KELLY. I said no. You want to take some pee?

DAIZY. No...I believe you.

KELLY. Good.

DAIZY. I'm glad.

KELLY. Me too. I –

(The intercom buzzer sounds.)

Shit.

DAIZY. Who's that?

KELLY. I got it. Don't worry. Be quick, all right? I have something to show you. *(She presses a button on the intercom.)* Hey –

EMILY. *(offstage)* It's me.

KELLY. Come up.

(She buzzes her in.)

DAIZY. On a Sunday, Kel?

KELLY. It'll be short, I promise.

DAIZY. I thought you were gonna take a break.

KELLY. I am. Soon as this is done.

(He glances at the table.)

DAIZY. She finished? Can I take a look?

KELLY. Later, okay? Trust me.

(**KELLY** *raises the gate. The elevator doors open, and* **EMILY** *enters.)*

EMILY. Hi. Hi Daizy.

DAIZY. *(putting on his pants)* Hey...

KELLY. Thanks for coming, Emily. On a weekend –

EMILY. Oh, please. Weekends are best. I'm excited. That was quick.

KELLY. We need to talk.

EMILY. Oh. All right. *(She pulls up a chair, sits.)* I don't want to monopolize your time, but – I'm glad you called. I was hoping...You'd get inspired. Some kind of break-through. I can't wait to see what you've done.

KELLY. Yeah.

EMILY. *(glancing at the table)* Is she..?

KELLY. I'm actually – I'm gonna have to give back your deposit, Emily...

EMILY. Really? What for?

KELLY. Because. I can't – do what you wanted me to do. Make her – the way you wanted. How you remember her. I'm sorry.

(**KELLY** *holds out some money.)*

EMILY. Keep it. Please. She's worth twice that, the way she is. Even unfinished. I'm thrilled to have her.

KELLY. I don't think I, uh – I'm not sure you understand.

EMILY. No?

KELLY. No, she's not "unfinished," she's – not for sale any-more, Emily. I'm keeping her.

(**EMILY** *glances at* **DAIZY**.)

EMILY. Well, no. I definitely don't understand.

KELLY. I'm sorry. I wanted to tell you in person. So I could explain.

EMILY. Yes, please. Explain.

KELLY. I can recommend another artist if that would be –

EMILY. I don't want another artist! *(beat)* Okay, look, I feel a little bit silly, getting upset over a doll. We're adults, right? I haven't completely lost perspective, but – We're talking about a likeness of my daughter, right? It isn't entirely yours to decide.

KELLY. Yes it is. She's mine. I made her.

EMILY. To my specifications. Legally, you know – just to start thinking about – It's a breach of contract.

KELLY. You don't have a contract.

EMILY. Sure I do. An oral one. I paid a deposit.

KELLY. I said I'd give it back.

EMILY. I don't want your money! I want what I paid for.

KELLY. Well, you'll have to sue me then.

DAIZY. I don't know if that's a good suggestion, Kel.

EMILY. *(takes a deep breath)* All right, look – I understand. People get attached to their work. Portrait painters. Kitchen contractors, for chrissake. Maybe I was too – demanding. Because I have so much respect for what you do, Kelly, and I thought – we were connecting a bit, on some level...So I figured you could use a little push. To realize your incredible gifts, but –

KELLY. Don't patronize me.

EMILY. I'm not. I'm not trying to. I just feel a bit – Bewildered. And – *lost*, honestly.

KELLY. Well, now you know how I feel. All the time.

EMILY. What does that mean?

KELLY. Forget it.

EMILY. Kelly?

DAIZY. Listen, I'm gonna have to ask you to leave now...

EMILY. What does that – I don't understand.

DAIZY. Emily..? Please? She's under a lot of pressure – We'll call you.

KELLY. Fuck you. Don't take her side.

DAIZY. I'm not taking sides.

KELLY. *(to* **EMILY***)* I'm not selling her to you. You don't deserve her.

(beat)

(EMILY *stands, takes her purse, and goes to the elevator, pushes the button.)*

KELLY. Here. Take your money...

EMILY. No.

KELLY. Take it, come on. Fucking take it.

(EMILY *doesn't respond.* **KELLY** *holds out the money.* **EMILY** *doesn't take it.)*

(The doors slide closed.)

(long pause)

DAIZY. Whoa...you okay?

KELLY. Yeah...

DAIZY. Wow. I wasn't expecting –

KELLY. No. Me neither.

DAIZY. You did the right thing though. Right? I think. Did you?

(KELLY *nods.)*

Yeah...that relationship was getting a little too – co-dependent or whatever? I can see that. Fuck it. You have more work than you can handle already, right?

KELLY. Hm.

(He grabs Baby Eva off the table.)

DAIZY. Guess we'd better decide what to do with the Chuckster here – *(He juggles Eva from hand to hand.)* Stuff her with candy and beat her with a broomstick? *(He swings her around by her legs.)* Rubber nunchucks? Touch football?

(He punts the doll across the room.)

(KELLY *gasps, snatches her off the floor.)*

KELLY. What are you, fucking NUTS, man?

(She holds the baby against her chest, bouncing her.)

DAIZY. Just fucking around...

KELLY. That wasn't funny!

DAIZY. *(surprised at her tone)* All right! Damn. I was just trying – to lighten the mood, you know. My bad. I know you worked hard on that thing. Uh...

KELLY. It's more than that.

(He looks at her, notices the way she's handling the doll.)

DAIZY. Kel...

KELLY. What?

DAIZY. What are you doing..?

KELLY. In terms of?

DAIZY. Why are you holding it like that?

*(**KELLY** stops bouncing.)*

KELLY. Like what?

DAIZY. Like...fucking *Rosemary*? *(beat)* Hey – I'm sorry I was so cavalier. Before. All right? It's beautiful, beautiful work, Kel. A *sculpture*, if you want to go all the way there, but –

KELLY. You didn't see her eyes, did you?

DAIZY. Yeah. I thought they were good. So?

*(**KELLY** holds Baby Eva up so he can see.)*

(long pause)

DAIZY. When'd you do that?

KELLY. Last night.

DAIZY. You didn't sleep?

KELLY. You were right. The eyes helped. Don't you think?

DAIZY. Yeah, she looks like you now.

KELLY. She is me.

DAIZY. Uh-huh. I'm – What?

KELLY. Look.

DAIZY. I am looking.

KELLY. Look harder.

DAIZY. This is tripping me out, okay? Just to let you know. You told me to let you know. Feel like I'm stuck in *The Shining* all of a sudden, and – "All work and no play makes Daizy really fucking freaked out."

KELLY. Don't you realize what this is, Daiz? She found me! She tracked me down. She found my website.

DAIZY. Who did?

KELLY. *(gesturing after* **EMILY***)* She "lost" her daughter twenty-some odd years ago? In Jersey? Doesn't that seem suspicious? She turns up now – In Queens?

DAIZY. You need help, Kel...

KELLY. That's just a coincidence? She happened to come here?

DAIZY. She wanted a doll. You make dolls. That's not a coincidence. That's a Google search.

KELLY. She was looking for me. She could have seen my picture, on the website –

DAIZY. How would she recognize you? Twenty years later?

KELLY. She would –

DAIZY. Honey, she's not looking for you.

KELLY. How do you know?

DAIZY. I know.

KELLY. How?

DAIZY. *(re: the doll)* Because. That isn't you.

KELLY. Who knows? I don't have baby pictures.

DAIZY. I think we should call somebody...

KELLY. Call somebody?

DAIZY. You need help, Kel.

KELLY. Why can't you just let me be happy? Ever. For one second.

DAIZY. I want you to be –

KELLY. So let me. I'm trying...it feels good, taking care of her.

DAIZY. But this isn't real. *(re: the baby)* That isn't real.

KELLY. She feels real to me.

DAIZY. "She" feels real to you because you're damaged, babe. I'm sorry, but – Kel – She feels like a spare tire.

KELLY. I can't feel her that way.

DAIZY. So let's tear it open. Look inside. You'll *see*. It's a coat of paint over rubber skin stuffed with silicone pellets and polyfill, remember?

(He takes a step toward her.)

KELLY. Maybe *you're* stuffed with polyfill. Maybe we should tear you open –

DAIZY. Honey...

KELLY. Fuck off, Daizy.

DAIZY. I want to help...

KELLY. You want to help me?

DAIZY. Yes. Please.

KELLY. You can't...You make it worse. *(beat)* You make me feel worse. You're so fucking normal...You've never had a crazy moment in your life. You're a hundred percent sane. Vanilla. With your stupid fucking name. Art school. Bullshit. The things you do all make sense. Good for you. You can't possibly understand. What I'm going through. It's beyond you. You make everything worse. So can you please get the fuck out of here? Right now? Please?

(He looks at her, starts to say something, and then turns and exits.)

*(**KELLY** stands there for a moment, alone, holding the doll.)*

(She puts it on the camera, turns on the camera, sits and rubs her eyes.)

(long pause)

KELLY. Just you and me now...

(She picks up one of her brushes.)

(Suddenly, Eva opens her eyes. On the projection, we see her move.)

*(**KELLY** gasps, drops her brush.)*

(She leans down to look closer.)

SCENE 7

(A coffee shop.)

(DAIZY sits alone at a table, waiting.)

(After a moment, EMILY enters.)

DAIZY. Hey – Thanks for coming.

(She sits.)

EMILY. You said it was urgent.

DAIZY. Yeah...sorry about the early phone call and every-thing. I couldn't sleep.

EMILY. What do you want?

(He takes a wad of cash from his pocket and lays it on the table.)

DAIZY. Brought your money.

EMILY. I told you. That isn't necessary.

DAIZY. Still. There's a guarantee. We'd feel much better if you took it.

(beat)

EMILY. Fine. Great.

(She takes the money.)

Is that all?

DAIZY. You can count it if you want.

(She stuffs it in her purse, stands.)

EMILY. You could have dropped it in the mail. I'm sure we all have better ways to spend our time. Some of us work.

DAIZY. Just a second...? Emily? Please...I didn't know who else to call.

(beat)

(She sits.)

I fucking hate dolls, you know?

EMILY. Really.

DAIZY. Yeah. I don't get the appeal, to be honest with you.

EMILY. I guess boys don't, usually.

DAIZY. No, that isn't it. I was completely gay as a six year-old. Listened to *Free to Be* all the time. I wanted a Cabbage Patch Kid, more than anything.

EMILY. But you didn't get one. And you were traumatized forever. Are we done?

DAIZY. No, I did. I got one. My dad went out, fought off the Christmas hordes, brought me home an African-American "Preemie" named Tabitha. To encourage diversity.

EMILY. Uh-huh. Weird.

DAIZY. Yeah. I had no idea what to do with her. This thing. She looked nothing like me. I couldn't make a connection. My friend Arthur? He got a boy doll. With a cowboy hat and a lasso. Named Dennis. It was completely fucking awesome.

EMILY. Must have been tough for you.

DAIZY. *(laughs)* Yeah, it was. It was. I shaved off all of Tabitha's hair. Mom made her a leather jacket and sparkly glove, circa *Bad*, which I thought was pretty fucking macho, and...I tried to like her. I tried, y'know? I pretended she was like me on the inside, just trapped. In that lady body. Poor Tabitha was the world's first passing tranny butch self-loathing Cabbage Patch doll. My parents were horrified. Their son, the racist, sexist, six-year-old. Eventually they gave in. I switched to G.I. Joe, you know. He-Man. Man-Tech.

EMILY. Boy dolls.

DAIZY. "Action figures".

EMILY. Right.

DAIZY. So now I'm sculpting dicks for a living. Go figure.

(She smiles.)

My point is, I guess I know how...*intense* people can feel – about these things. I mean – I don't want to trivialize. What you're going through...

EMILY. But?

DAIZY. But, yeah...I mean, you seem like a sensible adult. A successful – lawyer or whatever you are?

EMILY. Right. So you want to know..?

DAIZY. Why Kelly? Why dolls? What the fuck happened to you?

(She looks at him, trying to tell if he's mocking her.)

(She decides he isn't.)

EMILY. Well, I tried other things at first...

DAIZY. Like?

EMILY. Therapy. Valium.

DAIZY. Didn't help?

EMILY. No, they did...They did. I had a counselor. A support group. I divorced my husband. Slept with my shrink. Concentrated on my career. It's a *process*, you know, so – I'm not miserable, anymore, in any active, conscious sense, if that's what you're asking...

DAIZY. But?

EMILY. But, right. Well, it wasn't enough...for me. *(beat)* I weened Eva, you know, when she was six months old...I wanted to go back to work. To make partner. A year off would have killed my career. Put me in mom-limbo, permanently. And I couldn't stand pumping in the restroom, like a cow. Having the secretaries walk in on me. The slurping sound. So, we switched to formula. Martin gave her bottles during the day. My milk dried up. It was fine. Good. I had my body back. My work. But then, after we lost Eva...It came back. Pouring through my shirt at the office. I was swapping new pads in and out of my bra every two, three hours. Wearing heavy sweaters and jackets in the summertime...It was – like my body needed to go through these motions. *Use* the machinery that was just sitting there now, dormant...It went away, after a while. I thought, you know, time...Distance...It was working. Then last year, I started getting these hot flashes. And it all came rushing back. That *need*. I see babies in the park now, when I'm out jogging, and I want to touch them so bad, my fingers ache.

DAIZY. How come you never had another kid?

EMILY. *(smiles)* Too hard...Anyway, I met this woman, at the mall. This woman, she raved about Kelly. How much it had helped her. Given her a new way to cope. I thought, what the hell? I'd like to – go through the motions...It's embarrassing, obviously, to be in this situation. But I'm too old now to worry much about what other people think of me, so –

DAIZY. She thinks you're her mom.

(beat)

EMILY. I'm sorry, who?

DAIZY. Kelly. Thinks Eva's some kind of...self-portrait? She's got it into her head that you came looking for her. That she's been working on this thing for you, because you're –

EMILY. Her mother, the psychopath? *(beat)* My daughter died, all right? I didn't *disfigure* her.

DAIZY. You sure?

EMILY. Excuse me?

DAIZY. Can you prove it?

EMILY. No.

DAIZY. Why not?

EMILY. Because. It's private. And pointless. And I don't want to talk about it with you.

DAIZY. An act of God?

EMILY. Kind of. If you want to think of it that way. Personally, I don't believe in God so much anymore, but...

DAIZY. I could go to the police, you know. We could get a DNA test, I think –

EMILY. You want some DNA?

(She spits in his face.)

(beat)

(He wipes his cheek with a napkin.)

DAIZY. Listen...I'm pretty good at – not judging people, you know? I think they have reasons for all the crazy shit they do, most of the time. I won't think any less of you...

*(**EMILY** laughs.)*

What's funny?

EMILY. That you imagine I'd care. What you think.

DAIZY. So tell me.

EMILY. There's nothing to tell.

DAIZY. Babies don't just die, right? There must be some kind of a –

EMILY. Of course they do, like anybody. You have no idea how fragile, how –

(She stops, closes her eyes.)

DAIZY. I'm sorry...

EMILY. Are you?

DAIZY. Yes, I am. We don't have to talk about it anymore if you don't want to.

EMILY. *(laughs)* It's funny, you know. People like you... "Daizy". Pretend to be so empathetic. Confident you'll understand anything. Any horror. Like all it takes is being a nice, inoffensive kind of guy...And then, as soon as you're out of your depth, you fall back on – "I'm sorry." "My condolences." As if that means anything. Kelly has you figured out. It's obvious. Nothing bad has ever happened to you. So you think you're safe, because you're in a fucking *dinghy*. But you have nothing to offer someone who's drowning. You can't even swim.

(They look at each other.)

SCENE 8

(The loft.)

(KELLY *is at her table, working feverishly. The camera is off.)*

(The dolls from the shelves are scattered all over the room.)

(Emily's home video is playing silently on the projector, and we see Eva, as a toddler, taking her first steps.)

(We hear the sound of a baby crying, in the distance, echoing like it comes from inside a container.)

(KELLY *wipes her eyes – she hasn't slept in several days.)*

(The faint sound of the baby whimpering, trying to breathe...)

(KELLY *suddenly gags, claps a hand to her mouth.)*

(She runs to the bathroom.)

(We hear her retching into the toilet.)

SCENE 9

(later)

(Eva is lying on the table. The camera is off.)

(The apartment appears empty, but we can hear the sound of a faucet running in the bathroom, and see a trickle of water down the hallway.)

(After a moment, the elevator door opens and **DAIZY** *enters.)*

DAIZY. Kel? You home? We need to talk...

(He sees the tracks of water.)

(He glances into the kitchenette, bangs on the bathroom door.)

Hey – You in there?

(He tries the door. Locked.)

Shit.

(He throws his shoulder into the door, bounces off it.)

Ow! Fuck! Goddamnit.

(He holds his shoulder.)
Kelly? Can you open the door please? I hurt my arm.

(beat)

Open the door!

(He kicks the door several times. It doesn't open.)
Kelly!

(He looks around, takes a sculpting knife off Kelly's drafting table, and tries to jimmy the lock.)

(After a couple tries, it works. The door opens, and he goes inside.)

(offstage) Hey –

(The shower cuts off.)

(offstage) Hey, you all right? Honey, you okay?

(He reenters, carrying **KELLY**.*)*

DAIZY. You're fine. I got you now. Don't worry...

*(***KELLY** *is fully dressed, but soaking wet, her hair and clothes clinging to her.)*

(She clutches something tightly in her left hand.)

*(***DAIZY** *sets her down on the futon.)*

DAIZY. What happened? Jesus, you pass out or what?

*(***KELLY** *gives no response.)*

Kelly?

*(***DAIZY** *pulls her shirt up over her head. Small white scars from a long time ago are visible, standing out on her chest and stomach.)*

(He wraps her in a blanket.)

You hurt? Hurt anywhere?

*(***KELLY** *shakes her head).*

Okay. Just to let you know – I think I might have peed myself. You're scaring the crap out of me here.

KELLY. Me too...

DAIZY. Yeah? What happened? You all right?

*(***KELLY** *shrugs.)*

The apartment's flooded. Are you drunk?

KELLY. I needed to relax.

DAIZY. With the shower running? Your clothes on?

KELLY. It was fucking urgent.

*(Beat. ***DAIZY** *looks around the room.)*

DAIZY. What happened to your things?

(He sees the object in her hand.)

What's that?

KELLY. Nothing.

DAIZY. Let me see.

KELLY. No.

(He tries to pry open her fingers.)

KELLY. Stop –

DAIZY. You're using again..? Kelly?

(She laughs.)

KELLY. Using..?

DAIZY. God fucking damn it. Let me see!

KELLY. No!

(He grabs her wrist.)

DAIZY. I'm calling Pam and Herb. The cops. The hospital. Give it –

KELLY. No no no.

DAIZY. Fucking give it to me!

(They struggle for a moment, and then he wrests the thing away from her, looks at it.)

Jesus Christ...

(He sits back heavily on the floor.)

Kel? Is this – what I think it is, or –

KELLY. What do you think it is?

DAIZY. I don't know...Are you? Really..?

KELLY. According to the magic pee stick, which is more than 99.999999 percent accurate...Apparently.

DAIZY. Holy shit...*(beat)* I mean. Holy shit, right? You know? Kel, I mean – Congratulations?

KELLY. Ha!

DAIZY. No, I mean – Really. I'm serious, just took me a minute to –

*(**KELLY** scoffs.)*

Look, I know – Honey, you think I don't know this is fucking terrifying for you right now? To think about? I know that. It's a lot. To handle, at the moment. But it's good. I think, actually. It could be really, really good...

KELLY. How could it be good again?

DAIZY. Because! You know, it's amazing – we could teach it things. Like – how to finger paint and draw. Read books and shit like that. A family. And I think this could make you happy, honey, if you let it...

KELLY. That's a great reason to have a kid. Make yourself happy.

DAIZY. What other reason is there?

KELLY. How about because you're ready? You'd do a good job? You're motherhood material?

DAIZY. You are ready.

KELLY. *(laughs)* Yeah right...two seconds ago you thought I was OD-ing.

DAIZY. I was wrong.

KELLY. You were not wrong. I could have been, easily. I wanted to.

DAIZY. You didn't.

KELLY. Look what I did instead!

(She flips a switch on the projector, and we see Baby Eva, her eyes wide open, her face streaked with dirt and tears. She has a dozen carefully sculpted and painted bleeding puncture wounds in her chest and stomach, and her hands are burned, raw, bubbling.)

DAIZY. Jesus Christ, Kel...*(He switches off the projector.)* Uh... *(He picks up the doll.)* Okay...Look, I'm gonna take this out of here, right? I'll take it, so you don't have to think about – and put it somewhere safe, all right?

*(***KELLY*** makes an inarticulate sound in her throat, flies at him, and snatches Baby Eva away.)*

(She retreats to the corner, holding the doll to her chest.)

DAIZY. Kelly...

KELLY. I couldn't help myself! All right? Now you know. I'm a fucking basket-case, Daizy. I'd be dangerous to a little kid. I might *hurt* her. Imagine, if I did this to a *toy*, what I could do to a real person. A helpless fucking infant? Who needed to be fed? And have her diapers changed? Somebody who'd remind me of – Jesus, Daiz, I'm nuts! Look at me.

(He looks.)

DAIZY. Okay, yes, you're nuts.

KELLY. Ha...

DAIZY. But lots of people are. Believe me. I come from a very normal family, and they're worse. I know you. You would never hurt anybody.

*(**KELLY** gestures at the doll.)*

She isn't real, Kelly. That doesn't count. You made her. Maybe you just had to work through some shit, you know? Try it out. Doesn't Freud say anything about this type of –

KELLY. No.

DAIZY. No? Are you sure?

KELLY. Yes.

DAIZY. Well, he should have. Fucking idiot. I'll say it for him. This is subconscious – doll transference syndrome or some shit like that. It's not real. And if you have to like – act out some horrible fucking nightmare in your work, so you can – understand it and – deal with it. Good for you! It doesn't mean you'd do anything, in real life.

KELLY. How do you know?

DAIZY. I've been reading, okay...about dolls? Words have pictures next to them on the internet, which is really helpful for a guy like me.

*(**KELLY** laughs, sniffles.)*

And I saw this thing? About voodoo magic? How it isn't really used, you know, for the horror-movie type shit you see on TV. That's a racist stereotype. The witch doctors, in Jamaica? They make dolls of themselves sometimes. Their friends. Family members. People who are sick. Or unhappy. They make the doll all fucked up. Like – they'll put it in the oven if the person's got a fever. Or if she's got a headache, they'll ram a nail through the puppet's head. If she's sick, they'll wrap it in infected blankets. And then, you know, they take the doll out of the oven. They take off the blankets. They pull out the fucking nail, you know? Try to make the person better?

KELLY. You don't understand, Daiz...

DAIZY. But I'm trying! I'm trying to understand. I think you'd make a fantastic – a kid would be lucky as hell to have you for a mom!

KELLY. I'm not gonna subject a baby to this. All by herself? I can't.

DAIZY. She wouldn't be by herself though. She'd have us.

KELLY. What? To protect her?

DAIZY. That's what parents do, right?

KELLY. Not my parents. *(beat)* Look at me, Daiz. I'm supposed to be a mother? Have a baby? Me?

DAIZY. People do. Britney Spears.

KELLY. You know what I mean. I have a history.

DAIZY. That doesn't mean anything.

KELLY. It might. Cycles of abuse. You know, inherited mental illness. Maybe my mom was just like me. Maybe there's a gene, lurking inside my brain...a demented psycho Andrea Yates gene. Waiting to get triggered post-partum and drive my family off a fucking cliff.

DAIZY. You're not like that.

KELLY. How do you know?

DAIZY. I know you –

(The loud squawk of the door buzzer.)

(KELLY looks up at DAIZY.)

KELLY. Who's that..?

(DAIZY gets up and touches a button on the intercom.)

(panicked) Daizy? Who the fuck is at the door?

DAIZY. Kel...I need to say something here –

KELLY. About what?

DAIZY. I just want you to listen to me for a sec, all right?

KELLY. About fucking what?

DAIZY. I talked to Emily –

KELLY. You..?

DAIZY. Yes. I went and talked to her. About what happened...

KELLY. You talked to her? Who said you could – Who said you could talk?

DAIZY. I needed help. Thinking about you – Figuring this out.

KELLY. From her?

DAIZY. Yes. Because she needs help too, Kel. And I thought we could all –

KELLY. No.

DAIZY. Yes. Come on, listen –

KELLY. *(clutching Eva)* No no no no no...You make her go away.

(The elevator door opens, and **KELLY** *scoots back against the wall, her arms wrapped around Eva.)*

*(***EMILY** *enters, takes in the room, sees* **KELLY**, *crouched in the corner.)*

(beat)

(She approaches **KELLY**, *kneels next to her.)*

*(***KELLY** *shrinks away.)*

EMILY. Hey – I brought you some things...

(She digs in her purse.)

I thought you might need to see. Look. An obituary from the *Star Ledger*...Her hospital bracelet...A program from Eva's memorial...

*(***KELLY** *takes the paper, reads.)*

(long pause)

(She starts to cry.)

*(***DAIZY** *crouches down next to her.)*

DAIZY. Hey – Honey? You want to tell her?

KELLY. I'm not having any baby, Daizy...

DAIZY. Why not?

KELLY. I can't. Look at me. *(showing Baby Eva to* **EMILY***)* Look at what I did...

(beat)

*(***EMILY*** reaches for the doll.)*

*(***KELLY*** holds onto it for a second. And then slowly, lets her pull it away.)*

*(***EMILY*** swaddles the doll in a blanket.)*

*(***DAIZY*** puts his arms around* **KELLY***. They watch* **EMILY** *with the doll.)*

*(***EMILY*** smiles, rocks Eva gently, strokes her hair.)*

EMILY. *(humming Brahms' Lullaby:)* La da dum...da da dum... La da da da da da dah...La da dum...La da dum...La da da da da da da dah...

(The four of them sit there, together, as the lights fade.)

END OF PLAY.

ACKNOWLEDGEMENTS

I wrote *Reborning* in Juilliard's American Playwrights Program, and I'm deeply indebted to the mentorship of Marsha Norman and Chris Durang, and to the other brilliant writers in the room: Katori Hall, Sam Hunter, Nathan Jackson, Carly Mensch, Liz Merriwether, Emily Schwend, and Beau Willimon.

Kip Fagan brought his inimitable style, intelligence, and empathy to the play's first production. Greg Keller, Ally Sheedy, and Katherine Waterston gave depth and shading to the roles they originated. And Josh Costello and his cast at the San Francisco Playhouse helped me see the script with fresh eyes and brought the play finally and fully to life.

Phyllis Wender supported this play, as she does all my work, with ferocity, integrity, wit, and warmth. I feel grateful to have her in my corner.

Finally, my family – Bill Ayers, Bernardine Dohrn, Malik Dohrn, and Chesa Boudin – who inspire me with their commitment to children and to justice. And my wife, Rachel DeWoskin, who inspires me with her crazy brilliant mind. She had the idea, and all the ideas.

Lightning Source UK Ltd.
Milton Keynes UK
UKOW030610210213

206594UK00007B/182/P